WARNING

This book contains sexually explicit scenes and adult language. It may be considered offensive to some readers. This book is for sale to adults ONLY.

* * * * * * * * * * * * * * * * * * *

Please store your files wisely where they cannot be accessed by underage readers.

ISBN-13: 978-1987863246
ISBN-10: 1987863240

Other Books by Darla Dunbar:

<u>The Romeo Alpha BBW Paranormal Shifter Romance Series</u>

Amanda Walker thinks that she has a normal and boring life. That is until after her 24th birthday. Everything changes when she meets the man who says he was supposed to be her husband. Denying everything the man says, she fights him every step of the way. But after he kidnaps her, Amanda discovers that there are some things about her family that her parents kept a secret all these years. Among the history of the family she learns secrets she thought only happened in story books. Can Amanda tell the difference between truth and lies or is she this mysterious woman that holds the key to a legacy?

<u>Romeo Alpha Blood Lines Romance Series</u>

Twenty-four years have passed in relative peace for Amanda and Romeo. They've raised five children into adulthood and are thoroughly enjoying their lives as the Alpha King and Queen of the werewolves. At twenty-four, Sarina is just stepping into her powers and will be ripe for mating when her birthday comes in two weeks. What no one knows is the danger that lurks just outside their tight knit community. Romeo has made peace with the other clans and has enjoyed that peace, but it will all come crashing down around him when his oldest daughter comes of age to take a mate.

The Alpha Feud BBW Paranormal Shifter Romance Series

Eliza's life consisted of reporting on boring, crowd-pleasing events, like their country livestock fair. With the arrival of two handsome brothers, the lives of Eliza and her best friend, Melissa, are shaken to the core. For Eliza, the arrival of this new man becomes a test of her relationship with her current boyfriend, who she's been happily living with for over six years. Does Hayden, a complete stranger, really wield the power to make Eliza reconsider her relationship with Andrew?

The Alpha Packed BBW Paranormal Shifter Romance Series

Darlene has led a quiet life since suffering through a terrible break-up. She wants nothing more than to spend her time in front of the TV, away from any sort of trouble. But all that goes down the drain when handsome, rugged and rough Idris comes into her life. He is a werewolf on the lookout for his missing pack leader. Darlene quickly finds herself pulled towards this mysterious man and at the same time finds herself falling deeper and deeper into the world of the supernatural.

The Mind Talker Paranormal Romance Series

Ananda finds herself on the run and she's not alone. With help from Jared, a stranger that she just met, the two evade capture by an organization that is intent on hunting her kind. Ananda and Jared are able to read minds. When an unfortunate incident happened involving a disturbed individual that resulted in the death of his schoolmates, the secret organization decided to take action.

<u>The Leather Satchel Paranormal Romance Series</u>

Valtina is stuck in Middle World, unable to pass on to The Afterlife. In order to redeem herself from past deeds done, she must help bring romance back into the world and stop The Dark Side from destroying love in its entirety. Following orders issued by Ladaya and armed with a leather satchel filled with the appropriate tools and weapons, Valtina embraces each mission with enthusiasm.

Get the latest update on new releases from the author at:

https://darladunbar.com/newsletter/

This book is Part Eight of "<u>The Daemon Paranormal Romance Chronicles</u>"

Book 1 - The Awakening

Phoebe grew up not knowing her mother. The stranger, Apollo Mikos, claimed to know her mother. After that day, Phoebe's life would change forever.

Book 2 - The Shifter

Phoebe is surprised when her dog, Ace, shows up from nowhere. She is on a mission with Apollo to kill the Qilin. That is the only way that the true leader of daemons will emerge.

Book 3 - Forgotten

Juno has been stirring up trouble that has prolonged the infighting among the daemons. In order to get her to stop, Phoebe agrees to give up a year of her memories. But making deals with a siren is never a good thing. Without her memories, Phoebe's romantic relationship with Supay no longer exists. Instead, she leaves Supay for Apollo.

Book 4 - The Siren's Trap

The unsuspecting couple, Phoebe and Supay, made a deal with Juno to stop the infighting among the daemons. But at what price? An entire year was wiped clean from Phoebe's mind. Now Phoebe was with Apollo. Desperate to get her back, Supay considers Juno's new deal. Is it worth the price to pay for the dubious result? To win back Phoebe's love, Supay will need to be unfaithful to her.

Book 5 - Exposed

Hiding away in Peru, Supay and Phoebe start their own family, away from the chaos and the daemon infighting. Meanwhile, Apollo, heart-broken and lost, is lured into another one of Juno's schemes. Making deals with a siren never turns out right. If Apollo accepts the deal, the love of his life may resent him for the rest of his natural life. If he doesn't take the deal, she is lost to him forever.

Book 6 - The Beginning

As preparations for the war between daemons are underway, everyone must begin to choose. Siding temporarily with Apollo, Juno has a moment to look back on her life and figure out how she arrived at this moment. As she sifts through memories of the past, a specific dark stranger stands out. How far will young Juno go with her new love? More importantly, will her mother, Circe, discover the secret tryst?

Book 7 - The Treachery

Having broken the cardinal rule of the sirens, Juno must take action to save her own life and the life of her unborn child. In order to keep her secret safe from the sisterhood, she must kill her lover and conceal her shame. Will Juno betray the sisterhood and save her lover or will she remain loyal by slaying him instead?

Book 8 - Duplicity

Juno's mother, Circe, discovers her lies and gives her an ultimatum to fix everything. As Juno races against the clock to protect her loved ones from Circe, she makes a final choice that could leave her perpetually unhappy. Left to wander the world alone, Juno realizes that freedom means nothing if there is no one to share it with. The nature of Juno's vendetta—and the means she achieves it with—are finally revealed.

Book 9 - Reconnaissance

As Juno's hunt for the daemon's fortress unfolds, Apollo is left alone wondering if she will truly return to him. Will Juno be able to resist her base instincts? More importantly, will she be able to get to the fortress and return without being spotted? Discover how Juno's stealth mission works out.

Book 10 - The Interrogation

Juno tries to hide her rising fear in the presence of her captors. As her fear mounts, she holds on to the hope that Phoebe or Supay will take pity on her. Before that can happen, she has to come clean to Supay about her past. Could he possibly forgive her for what she has done? Will Juno remain faithful to Apollo or will her siren urges take over? Discover how the confrontation with Supay unfolds.

The Daemon Paranormal Romance Chronicles

Duplicity

Book Eight

By Darla Dunbar

Copyright Revelry Publishing 2015

Table of Contents

Chapter One

IT HAD been several months since the trauma around Supay and Yossele had died down. From that time on, Juno had carefully avoided seeing Supay. She spent most of her days at home with her new-born daughter, Maia. Wrapped up in the joys of motherhood, she had managed to put the tragic events out of her mind temporarily.

Turning a corner, Juno sighed in relief. Circe must be out for the day. Soon enough, Juno's training ought to begin. Hopefully, she would be able to spend more time with her daughter before that happened. Upon hearing the gurgles and giggles of Maia, Juno returned to the nursery. She picked her daughter up, sat down on a rocking chair in the room and began to play with her.

"You look just like daddy," she cooed as she tickled Maia under the chin. Her gentle tickles were rewarded with a beautiful smile. "We'll see him someday, my love. We just have to wait for the right time." Juno held her daughter closer and started to rock gently back and forth. Before long, the motion would help Maia return to dreamland. Sighing in happiness, she relaxed for a few moments. Without Circe here, she could stop being so tense.

Juno set her daughter back into the crib and tiptoed quietly out of the room. Turning around, she ran into Circe. Juno smiled pleasantly as she tried to hide her surprise. "I did not expect to see you here, Mother. How has your day been?" she asked.

Circe motioned for her to follow her to the kitchen. "My dear, I am afraid that it is time for you to finish your training. I have just the dress in mind."

Confused, Juno followed her into the kitchen. On the table, a button-up black dress was carefully laid out with matching heels. She looked at Circe inquisitively. "What do you mean… *finish my training?*"

Shaking her head, Circe handed Juno the shoes to try on. "It is not quite over with. A siren's training is unique to each siren. Since you reached adulthood a year ago, I had waited patiently for you to take your first lover. Like every young siren, you were unable to control yourself and soon were with child. Your actual training started on the night that you had to end the affair. Sirens do not love. We manipulate and we wreak havoc on the humans around us. Your first test was to do so with the man that you loved. I had thought at the time that you had done an admirably good job. Unlike many young sirens, you were able to manage the matter without leaving your fingerprints upon the results."

Circe sat down and crossed her legs delicately. "Unfortunately, my suspicion about the parentage of your child was confirmed by what I just heard in the nursery. You still have to end things with Supay. If you are able to ruin your relationship well enough for him to never return, I will allow your daughter to live."

Juno's eyes flashed angrily and fear crept into her mind. She consciously tried to control her thoughts. Somehow, she had to get free of the siren world. She would never be able to love who she wished or raise her daughter if sirens were involved. For the moment, her primary focus would be to ensure the safety of her child. "What will happen to Maia if I do this?" she asked in a cold monotone. Never again would Juno let Circe realize her pain.

Shrugging, Circe reached over to help Juno undress and put on the black dress. "Your daughter is old enough to be adopted out. Traditionally, a daughter is always raised by an unknown siren. It ensures that every member of our sisterhood works with each other and remains loyal." Circe pulled the dress over Juno's head. "It really is the best way. Once you have these romantic notions about love and motherhood banished from your mind, you will be able to do great things. Ending things with Supay will be your final test. If you can do that well enough, you are free to leave me and make your way in the world."

As she buttoned up the last button on the dress, Circe kissed Juno gently on the cheek. The slim, youthful figure of Juno reminded Circe of how she had once felt in the same situation. For a moment, Circe felt sympathy for her adopted daughter. Crushing these romantic notions was the most difficult part of growing up, but it was necessary. Someone who loved deeply and truly was at risk—and sirens were never weak.

"Good luck, Juno. I'll pack your bags while you're gone and send off your daughter. When you return, you can take your bags and go wherever you wish."

Juno's eyes widened. Despite her vow to never show feelings to Circe, she struggled. "Maia? You can't take her. She's my daughter."

Shaking her head, Circe began to walk from the room. "Come with me and I'll let you say good-bye. I'm not as cruel as my adopted mother was—you can kiss her good-bye before you leave. But don't think of trying anything. There are many sirens in the world and we can manipulate anyone we please. You would never be able to run away with her and live."

Returning to the nursery, Juno stood nearby and watched the sleeping figure of her daughter. Small sighs permeated the room as Maia breathed deeply in her sleep. Leaning her head against the door frame, Juno struggled to keep her face blank. She knew that Circe was nearby and did not want Circe to see her pain. Someday, she would find Maia again and try to repair things with Supay. Until that time, she had to ensure that the people she loved the most were safe. The easiest way to do that was to follow Circe's orders and let Maia go.

Juno turned from the nursery. She would not say good-bye. If she merely touched her daughter, she would break into tears and be unable to continue. Glancing over at Circe, Juno nodded. "I'm ready. Arrange the transportation. I need to get to the mines."

Chapter Two

Several hours later, Juno finally arrived in La Rinconada, Peru. She gazed around at the snow-capped mountains before focusing on the village. The streets were filthy. Few, if any, houses appeared to have running water or plumbing. Stepping around a beggar on the sidewalk, she looked around for a bar, restaurant or main office. Somehow, she needed to find out where Supay was located and end things.

Juno finally found a bar after wandering the streets. Unlike the buildings that surrounded it, this structure seemed to be fairly clean. Swinging the bar door open, Juno entered the room. As she stepped inside, the bartender looked up. "Whisky and cola," she said before sitting down.

She surveyed the room while seated on the stool. A few dirty miners had already taken up residency at a table in the back. From the sounds of it, their Inca Cola was strongly mixed with alcohol and their poker game was well underway. Juno wrinkled her nose. This town was one of the most disgusting places she had ever imagined. When Supay said his father believed in teaching him the value of hard work, he meant it. This was not his father's copper mine. Instead, La Rinconada was a town on the top of the Andes that mined for gold.

Outside, she could see workers whose hands were covered with mercury residue.

With a shudder, Juno placed some sols on the counter to cover the cost of her drink. Leaning back, she sipped from her glass pensively. Soon enough, she would need to find Supay. As one of the cleanest bars in town, this seemed like the most likely place.

The door of the bar opened and a young, white man walked in. Ambling over to her, he tilted his cowboy hat amicably before removing it. "Why, hello, darling," he drawled.

Raising her eyebrow, Juno gazed at him with a bemused grin. With his hat off, the strange man's brilliant green eyes were easy to see. She reached out her hand. "A pleasure. I am Juno, Mr...?" She waited.

He smiled and his white teeth flashed merrily at her. "I'm Will. Nice to meet you, Juno. What brings you to town?"

Lowering her eyes demurely, Juno spoke softly. "I came to find an old friend. You look quite different from anyone else in town. Why are you in La Rinconada?"

In front of her, Will shrugged and leaned forward. His muscles rippled slightly as he folded his arms above the counter top. Without making a conscious decision about him, Juno's mind instantly started to fantasize about wrapping his arms around her. She struggled to refocus her mind on what Will was saying.

"Well, little Miss, I came out to this La Rink-honda to give some mining estimates. Some locals did it, but no one trusts it. They also hired some Chilean guys to check it out, but they're still not happy. Their bad luck is my good fortune. This time around, they figured on hiring out the task to an American. I flew down here last week and, man, are you ever a sight for sore eyes." He grinned and reached out for her drink. "You want another? I'm buyin'."

Juno smiled. While she waited to end things with Supay, Will could certainly take her mind off of things. "Sure," she said. She reached her hand across the counter and found his. Gently, she began to stroke each finger individually. Across from her, Will shivered at the sensation that moved across his body. Each touch from Juno brought an instant pleasure to his nerves.

Will closed his eyes. "I think that the last five minutes have made this entire trip worthwhile." He opened his eyes again and motioned toward the door. "You ready to get out of here?" he asked. In front of them, the bartender plunked down the next round.

Picking up her drink, Juno tossed her head back and downed the glass. Will followed suit and stood up. Before he could turn toward the door, Juno pulled on his shirt collar and brought him close to her face. The sweet scent of liquor on her breath mingled with her natural jasmine scent as she pulled him closer. With her foot, she nudged his cock through the clothing. Will held back a moan as he waited for her next move. Juno unbuttoned the first button on her shirt slowly as she tried to buy time. A little bit of pleasure would take the sting off of today's task, but it could also make her job easier. If they remained at the bar, Supay would undoubtedly find out about this tryst. Things would be over between them without her ever needing to explain.

Juno smiled to herself. This would work perfectly. Turning around, she motioned for him to follow her to the back of the bar. Without waiting to see if he followed, she opened the emergency exit and stepped outside. Behind her, Will stepped through the door. In the alleyway, nothing was visible except for them.

Grinning in delight, Will started to say something. Before he could speak, Juno began to unbutton her dress in front of him. One by one, the buttons opened to reveal the entire front of her body. Hypnotized by her movements, Will found it difficult to say anything or even move. Her beauty was surreal and unlike any woman that he had ever been with. Stepping forward, he kneeled at her feet and spread her legs. Using his fingers, he spread her lips and started to gently play with her clit. Above him, Juno moaned in pleasure. This was just what she needed in order to finally unwind. Will slipped his fingers inside of her and groaned. She was unbelievably tight and wet. Foreplay was nice, but he needed more.

Standing up, Will pulled her head back by her hair. With her face tilted toward him, he leaned in and kissed her. Against his chest, he could feel the points of her nipples sticking out from her supple breasts. He reached his other hand down to her breasts and fondled each one in turn. Nudging her against the wall, Will stepped back and admired her body. Juno's long, slender legs met at the base of her hourglass figure. In front of her, Will began to unbutton his shirt.

Half-naked, Juno watched unabashedly as Will eyed her body. He stripped his shirt off and his tanned skin gleamed in the bright light. Unbuckling his pants, he stepped closer to Juno and shoved her against the wall. Wrapping her legs around his waist, he thrust inside her with one clean motion. Juno moaned as he entered her again and pulled him closer. Using her legs and the wall as leverage, she pushed her hips into his. Each thrust brought her another round of pleasure and urged her onward to the brink. Driven mad with desire, Will pumped his cock into her as quickly and thoroughly as possible. Each thrust felt like it was impaling her as Will entered deeper and deeper. In an instant, the pleasure was suddenly too much. Crying out in pain, pleasure and desire, Juno began to orgasm around Will. The clenching of her body around his urged him closer. Within several thrusts, Will groaned in sweet agony as he released himself inside of her.

Pressing himself fully against her body, Will ran his hand along her stomach and breasts. Looking into her eyes, he started to kiss her passionately. Instead of growing softer, he felt his cock harden again. Juno's legs tightened around his body and he realized that she was ready for a second bout. As he began to thrust into her for another round, the back door opened. Will started to move out of sight, but Juno just pulled him deeper inside of her.

Looking over, Juno smiled sweetly. "Supay, you're here, darling." she drawled with an accent that she had copied from Will. As the door shut loudly, Supay stood dumbfounded and gazed at Juno.

Glancing back and forth between them, Will quickly realized that he was not needed. Touching his hat brim as a sign of respect, he grabbed his shirt. "I guess I'll just skedaddle on out of here then." He tipped his brim toward Juno. "A pleasure, little lady," he winced as soon as he said it. Somehow, he managed to always say the least appropriate thing.

As Will left, Juno collapsed against the wall of the building and reached for her purse. Several feet away from her, Supay was still aghast and unable to respond. She pulled out a cigarette and lit it daintily. While she waited for Supay to come to grips with reality, she tried to rearrange herself. Her normal straight, neat hair was messed up from Will pulling on it during sex. Juno's dress remained completely open in front, but she did not care. Instead, she propped herself comfortably against the wall and crossed one leg over the other. Taking another drag from her cigarette, she glanced over at Supay. "The bartender told you I was out here?"

Supay nodded. "What is this? I have not seen you or even spoken to you for months. This is how you wanted to see me again?" he asked.

Juno did her best to smile seductively. It was harder to be cruel than she thought. "Well, I am a siren, you know. My training is almost complete. I thought I would stop by just to say good-bye."

Glancing at her figure, Supay collapsed against the wall next to her. He could not understand where the sweet, innocent girl he loved had disappeared to. For many nights, he had kept himself warm with thoughts of returning to Juno one day. After the death of his brother, there had been very few things that had ever brightened his mood. "What happened to you?" he asked as his nose wrinkled in disgust.

She attempted to shrug nonchalantly. Flicking the ash from the tip of the cigarette, she put it out with the heel of her shoe and stood up. "Nothing happened. I just know who I am now. The woman you were in love with was a siren and still is. You can't expect anything better from me." Unbeknownst to Supay, Juno secretly winced as she said this. The pain he was going through was too much, but she could not allow herself to lessen it. "I sleep with men to gain what I want and to satiate myself. That's who I am." To avoid seeing his reaction, she turned away from Supay. She could hear him stand up slowly.

"Well, if that's what you want, you do not have to worry about dealing with me ever again." Giving her one last glance, Supay turned to go. His insides writhed in disgust as he realized that the woman he had been with, his first love, was just a mirage.

Juno turned toward him to stop him. Her impulsive action caused Supay to look at her inquisitively. "I just..." she faltered. She had to keep up the charade somehow. Moving her leg closer to him, she allowed her thigh to rub against the side of his leg. Despite his disgust, Supay felt himself growing hard. He turned to leave. "Wait, Supay. Don't you just want one last fling together?" Leaning closer to him, she ran her lips along his ear and nibbled slightly on the lobe. Supay shivered in pleasure, but prevented himself from responding in any other way. Reaching her hand toward his belt, she unbuckled it and managed to unbutton his pants. With a jerk, his member swung free of its constraints. Juno raised an eyebrow. "It is still possible to want what you despise, you know."

Unwilling to respond, but not able to leave, Supay stood immobile as she ran her hand down his cock. Drops of pre-cum already moistened the surface of the head as she brought him fully to attention. Grinning maliciously, she pressed one of her feet onto the wall for support. Her cunt was just at the height of his throbbing member. Bringing herself closer to him, Juno allowed his head to feel how moist and welcoming she was. In response, Supay reached for her hips to pull her onto him. Juno grinned again and arched her hips away. She was not going to allow herself to be taken so easily.

Again, she brought her hips close to his and slid down around his cock. She covered just his head in a delightful, taunting tease. Supay groaned. His morals, feelings and personal thoughts did not matter anymore. He needed Juno one last time. In the secret recesses of his mind, Supay promised himself that this would be it. From this day forward, he would never think of the siren again.

Gazing into his eyes, Juno could see desire clouding out Supay's better impulses. Thrusting her hips down hard against his, she allowed him to enter her fully. With a groan of pleasure, Supay returned the thrust. Sinking to the ground, he pulled her along with him.

Above his body, she rocked in splendid abandon as he pulsed and throbbed inside of her. The sweetness of this last encounter was not lost on Juno and she moved rapidly as her desire mounted within her. Faster and faster, her hips moved against his delicious body until Supay began to orgasm. She continued to move against him until her body had wrung every drop of his orgasm from him. Only at this moment did she start to come. Throwing her head back, she screamed in pleasure from the wave of feelings that washed over her body and groaned with the agony of the separation that was about to arrive. As her moans lessened, she realized again where she was. Lovingly, she looked down at Supay and leaned in to kiss him. He turned his head and she remembered again why she was here.

Getting into character again, Juno pulled herself off of Supay and started to button her dress. Supay remained, stunned, where she had left him. As he came to his senses again, he scurried to clothe himself again. Glancing over at her, his repulsion was evident. Juno was not the woman he thought she was. An idealist at heart, Supay could never bring himself to be with such a despicable creature. Without saying another word to her, he left the alleyway and her life forever.

Chapter Three

After her experience with Supay, Juno fell to pieces. She was now, officially, a siren, but it meant nothing to her. Even the knowledge that Supay and Maia were safe brought her no comfort. She wandered the world like a ghost and did her best to ignore the people around her. Although she struggled to control her urges as a siren, it was often too much for her and temptation beckoned around every corner. At long last, Juno found herself in a lonely ashram in India. For several months now, she had devoted herself to meditation and yoga. It seemed to be helping her control her urges temporarily. Instead of needing sex every few days, she was able to go up to a month without succumbing to desire. Unfortunately, the longer she spent without sex seemed to heighten her need for it. When she did finally give in, Juno was lost for days in a world where eroticism and S&M were just child's play.

Relaxing underneath a meditative tree, Juno tried to calm her mind. It had been three weeks since her last fling and she could feel the passion rising in her body yet again. Meditation was not going to be enough. Standing up, she began to walk outside of the ashram and followed a riverside trail. In a lonely, rock-strewn spot, she spotted an old, blind man. Walking up to him, she said "Hello."

The old man heard her speak and unfolded his legs. Reaching out his hand, his sightless eyes looked cheerily at her. "Juno, I was wondering when you would arrive?"

Juno pulled her hand back in surprise. "How do you know who I am? No one calls me by that name here."

The tiny man chuckled as he clasped his hands together. "I know everything about you, my dear. Your troubles, your love and your current problems are all just a drop in the bucket. If you need help, I am here to help you satisfy your heart's greatest desire."

Sighing, Juno sat next to the old man. He was undoubtedly a daemon of some sort. "Well, we'll see. If you can tell me what my dreams are, I will allow you to help."

Next to her, the man picked up her hand again. His gnarled fingers traced upon the outline of her palm. "I see. This will do quite nicely." Reaching under his white shirt, he pulled out an unusual necklace. Placing it around her neck, he said a few words in Arabic under his breath. "There, my dear," he patted her shoulder gently. "This will help bring about what you want."

Juno fingered the necklace and raised an eyebrow. Next to her, the man chuckled yet again. "Don't worry, it will help. If you wear this, you will end up living out your life in love with Apollo or Supay. I have a few short directions that you must follow to ensure everything succeeds, but after that, the future will be up to you."

Juno's breath caught in her throat as she realized that he was serious. "Supay or Apollo?" she asked. She had never even heard of a man named Apollo.

The old man nodded again. "It is fated that you shall be with one of the men or the other," he said, chuckling. "You are in luck, however. At this moment, there is a woman named Phoebe who is also fated to be with one of these two men. Her twin sister was intended to be the partner for the other man, but her early death changed the course of fate. To remedy this dilemma with destiny, you are to take her place and a siren will actually fall in love." Laughing, he patted her arm again. "I never thought I would live to see the day. If you are willing and ready to take on your fate, then come and study with me. As your mentor, I will teach you how to bring your dreams and destiny to life."

Chapter Four

It did not take very long for the old man to convince her to study under him. Over the course of several months, he taught her how to deny her siren self and seek her ultimate goals in life. Through his guidance, she used the necklace to travel back in time to the naming ceremony of the Qilin. With the spells she learned from Circe, Juno was able to flip the ba gua stones each time so that the little child was named Qilin. With this task complete, she returned to the old man to receive his last word of guidance.

Striding confidently next to the river, Juno appeared like a goddess in the dim light of twilight. Her hips swayed with their characteristic softness as she stepped gingerly between the sharp stones. At long last, she arrived next to the old seer. Holding out her hand, she dropped the necklace into his lap.

"My task was successful, old mentor. The child has been named the Qilin and should be as old as I am now." Sweeping her skirt out around her, Juno sat against the rocks.

The seer grinned. "Everything is ready, then. For the remainder of the story to play out, you must tell Apollo that the Qilin is now residing in San Francisco. Also, you will need to notify him about the potential powers that Phoebe possesses. She could be a great help to him in his journey." He cocked his head to the side as he thought. "If I am correct, Supay has already figured out that Phoebe will be needed in the hunt for the Qilin. He always was an intelligent boy."

Juno winced slightly. Hearing the name of Supay caused too many painful feelings to return. "Is that it? What happens after I finish these last steps?" she queried.

Shaking his head, the ancient seer shrugged. "There is no telling. Each path has slightly different outcomes at first. Just follow your instincts as a siren and you should be able to come out on top. After today, you will no longer need me, my child." He patted her on the head.

Bowing her head in respect, Juno bowed slightly from her waist before she stood up. "Thank you, sir," she whispered as she stepped away.

The waters of the scrying basin stirred unpleasantly as Juno drew her focus away from the memories. She waved her hand along the top of the water. One by one, the memories of her youth with Supay, early love and the seer disappeared among the ripples. Leaning back, she exhaled sharply. It had been a long path that she had taken to arrive at this castle.

Standing up, she walked slowly around the room. Since that evening so long ago, she had never seen the seer again. She had tried to end the relationship between Phoebe and Supay, but nothing had worked. Instead, she had thrown her energy into fighting them in the daemon war. Although she had promised not to directly engage in fighting, her assistance was invaluable for the Roman side. Juno shuddered. Out of all the daemons on earth, she and Apollo had had to work with the Romans. Their close ties and history with the Greek daemons had left bad feelings that had never truly stopped.

Reaching for a silk robe that she had left in the room, Juno wrapped it around herself and peered out the window of the tower. Below her, the troops were still running through practice drills. On the settee, Apollo slept heavily. She eyed him curiously. Over the recent months, she had wondered if he had developed more than a passing interest in her. It was a curse to be so attractive—it made it difficult to know if someone was truly interested in her or if it was just her sensual nature that drew them into her web. Despite this lack of certainty, she had felt the stirring of something more between them. Both cast aside by their former lovers, they had bonded first in bed and now as friends. Perhaps there would be something more to their relationship.

Returning to the settee, Juno stroked Apollo's head. How wonderful it must be to have such a simple life. Apollo did not know about her past history with Supay or that she had a daughter somewhere in the world. Juno ran her fingers through his flaxen hair. Somewhere, Maia existed and was probably about seven years old. Her hair would be the opposite color of Apollo's. With Juno's raven hair and Supay's dark complexion, Maia probably had midnight tresses around her face. Juno sighed. She would give anything to have Maia back, but she could not find her. Each time she looked for her in the scrying basin, emptiness appeared.

Beneath her hand, Apollo stirred. His eyes looked up sleepily at her as he kissed the inside of her wrist. "Why are you still up, Juno? Do you want to share my bed with me tonight?" he asked.

Juno nodded. "Yes, Apollo. I think that I will sleep in bed with you tonight." Wrapping her arms around his neck, she allowed Apollo to sweep her slender figure into his arms. Waving her hand behind her, Juno whispered an incantation and every candle in the room extinguished in an instant. Holding her body tightly against his, she relaxed finally into a deep, dreamless sleep.

-To be continued in Book 9-

If you enjoyed this title, I would appreciate your leaving a review of the book. Good reviews encourage an author to write as well as help books to sell. Good reviews can be just a few short sentences describing what you liked about the book without having a spoiler. If you could spend 30 seconds writing a review, I would appreciate it: you can review this title right now at your favorite retailer.

Here is a preview of the **next story** you may enjoy:

21

Reconnaissance - The Daemon Paranormal Romance Chronicles, Book 9

WAKING UP early in the morning, Juno gazed around the room. The cold walls of the castle stood in stark contrast to Apollo's blonde hair. Wearily rubbing her eyes, Juno rolled over and started to get out of bed. Next to her, Apollo struggled sleepily to pull her closer. Juno smiled and stepped away from the bed.

Putting on a robe, she waved her hand across the surface of the scrying basin. After revisiting the memories of her past, she had tried to see across time to the present. She needed to know what Phoebe, Supay and the Greek daemons were preparing to do. Despite her many attempts at scrying across the oceans, she could not get the present to reveal itself to her. The only reasonable answer was that the Greek daemons had chosen to block their activities from prying eyes, but Juno hoped that this was not the case. If she was not able to scry, she would have to go straight to the source to gather intelligence on the opposing side's forces.

Gazing into the ebony basin, few images appeared on the surface of the water. Shifting her gaze slightly, Juno switched between images of the Roman preparations to families cooking breakfast. Nothing appeared in the basin that seemed even remotely connected to the Greeks.

Leaning back heavily, Juno sighed. Her only task with the Romans was to gather intelligence. She had made a deal with Supay and Phoebe that she would not actively participate in the daemon war or stir up trouble.

This was the only thing that she could do to stay involved. Glancing over at Apollo, Juno sighed again. This was also the only way for her to stay near Apollo.

Wandering over to the window, Juno looked out over the preparations. The many archers positioned along the wall were unnerving enough. Last night, she had been told that an offensive plan was being readied. Although the Roman daemons wanted to keep the fighting quiet on the island of Sicily, they had no compunctions about drawing attention in Crete. Here, they would use archers, boiling tar and daggers to defend the castle. Over on the island of Crete, they were willing to use any manner of mortar, machine gun, mine or pistol. It was not looking good for Supay and Phoebe. Juno snorted. Not that she cared about Phoebe, but it would be heart wrenching to see anything happen to Supay.

A sound behind her indicated that Apollo was starting to wake up. Running her hands through her hair, Juno approached the bed. Slowly opening his eyes, Apollo caught sight of Juno and smiled. "There's my lovely lady," he murmured as he pulled her in for a kiss. Over the last few weeks, Apollo and Juno had grown increasingly close. What started as a simple, physical fling had transformed into something more. As of yet, Juno was not entirely sure how she felt. After her youthful romance with Supay years ago, she had forsworn any type of love or romantic entanglements. In reality, she had almost militantly stuck to the siren's code to never fall in love and only have sex for enjoyment or manipulation. During the last few weeks, she had enjoyed the closeness of her relationship with Apollo and the blossoming friendship.

If you enjoyed this sample then look for **Reconnaissance - The Daemon Paranormal Romance Chronicles, Book 9**.

Here is a preview of **another story** you may enjoy:

VALTINA SAT under a tree in Middle World,
observing the spirits around her. She'd been scanning
the faces of those who passed ever since Ladaya had
told her that her soul-mate was also stuck in Middle
World. She tried to sense his spirit, but as her mentor
had warned, she hadn't recognized him yet. Valtina
contented herself to sitting still and watching as the
others moved about. Like her, many had been enlisted
to fight in the war against evil. Middle World was
frequently filled with visitors from The Afterlife.
Generals, like Ladaya, popped in to give instructions
and updates to their soldiers. Valtina hadn't seen
anyone she recognized, though several of her friends
had already moved on.

As Valtina waited she thought about her mission.
The last one had been more difficult than the previous
one, as she'd had to break the spell of a succubus. And
Ladaya had warned her that all varieties of monsters
were fighting for the other side. She wondered what
kind of danger she would encounter next. Valtina's
thoughts were interrupted when Ladaya appeared
before her. She was frazzled, and seemed to be on the
verge of tears.

"Ladaya! What's happened?" Valtina asked in a
panic.

"I've just been observing," Ladaya sobbed, "the
mist… the black mist of evil… it's growing. I watched

it spread before my eyes. Oh Valtina, I don't know what we're going to do."

"Do you know what's making it spread so quickly?"

"We do. One of our under-covers reported in yesterday, and confirmed our worst fear. The driving force behind the other army is a creature that was believed to be a thing of legend. No one in my time, or the times of those before me, has ever encountered one. It is a thing so evil it cannot be killed. Part demon, part witch, she's rumored to be the spawn of a warlock and something very unnatural he conjured in his bedroom. Her powers are innumerable, and, I'm afraid, impossible to defeat. She's bred a wraith army; their sole purpose is to steal every soul on Earth. As you know, without a soul, one cannot feel love. If we don't stop them soon, it will all be over." Ladaya sighed.

"This creature… you don't mean a Mystic?!" Valtina asked with alarm.

"I'm afraid so." Ladaya nodded. "They call her Morgonda. We're quite certain she's the one who organized the monsters against us. Her goal is to rid the world of living creatures, and reign as Queen of the monsters.

"What can I do?" Valtina asked quickly. "How can we defeat them? Tell me how, Ladaya. Surely we need everyone focused on this right now. I can fix people's love lives once we've defeated them!"

"Valtina, I appreciate your offer. But it's important that we take advantage of each spirit's strengths. We have others who are more fitted to destroying evil, and you are too valuable in your area for us to risk you! But be aware, the wraiths can see you. Remember, their sole purpose is to steal souls… As you are nothing but a soul, you'd be an easy job for them. But, as usual, should you encounter one, help will appear."

"That's ridiculous, Ladaya," Valtina argued. "Don't the 'qualified' spirits have more important things to do than rescue me? Tell me how to take them out myself." she insisted.

Ladaya sighed. "Really, Valtina, I don't want you anywhere near them. There are rules for a reason, and you are no exception. And I believe that's one of the things you're in Middle World to work on? Following DIRECTIONS?" Ladaya reminded her sharply. Valtina sighed. It was true that in all of her lifetimes, she'd had a bit of a problem following the rules. Even really important rules she'd ignore, just for the sake of ignoring them. The Supreme Ruler in The Afterlife felt she needed some more practice in listening to authority before she moved on.

"I'm sorry, Ladaya. You're right," Valtina conceded. "What are my instructions? What's my next mission? The faster I get started, the faster I can move on to the next one, right?" She smiled.

Ladaya softened. "Well, as I told you, humans are spreading the evil almost as quickly as the monsters. Morgonda has sent these humans helpers, in the form of tricksters. They make sure the humans' plans fall into place, and that the plans of those around them fall apart.

I'm afraid they've been at work since long before we knew of The Dark Side's plans. The couple I'm sending you to next has been affected by a trickster for five years. They're a mismatched couple, you see, put together by their fathers as a part of a master business plan. The fathers sold their souls to a demon years ago, in exchange for success in their law firm. One man pressured his son to follow in his footsteps… the other did the same to his daughter. It seemed only natural to the two men that their children should marry, and keep the fortune within the two families. Claudia, the wife, fell in love with a man she met as an undergrad. Albert was smart and handsome, but seeking a teaching degree, which Claudia's father thought beneath his daughter. Sebastian, the husband, hasn't met his soul-mate yet. They were supposed to get together three years ago. So far, she hasn't encountered evil yet, and is still waiting for him.

"The trickster attached to Claudia and Sebastian's fathers put many obstacles in Albert's way, making it seem as if his relationship with Claudia was a lost cause. The trickster also made sure that Sebastian was in the right place at the right time to comfort Claudia after Albert disappeared. Then, the trickster inspired lust between the two. As soon as their fathers realized they were sleeping together, they insisted upon a wedding. The trickster was still doing his job, and inspiring lust between the couple. He's been dealt with, and now we need you to break up Sebastian and Claudia, and reunite them with their soul-mates," Ladaya finished.

"Consider it done, Ladaya," Valtina promised. "I'll return soon. I pray I come back to good news."

"That makes two of us." Ladaya smiled sadly.

The white fog enveloped Valtina and transported her to Claudia and Sebastian's townhouse. Valtina arrived early on a Saturday afternoon, and found the couple in separate rooms of the house. Claudia sat in the living room, absentmindedly watching a week's worth of recorded television. Valtina entered her mind for a moment. "What in the world has come over me?" Claudia thought. "He's my husband. I MARRIED him for Christ sake. Why am I suddenly looking at him like he's my brother? What am I going to do?"

Valtina felt sorry for Claudia. She didn't realize that she'd been under the influence of a trickster. All she knew was that suddenly, she wasn't attracted to her husband anymore. Valtina could read that Claudia still loved Sebastian very much, but not in a sexual way. The woman was fighting anxiety over what she would do the next time Sebastian propositioned her. "I just can't do it," she kept thinking to herself over and over again. "But why can't I just do it?" Valtina wanted to take the anxiety from Claudia, but felt it may be best to let it work to her advantage. She left the woman in the living room and glided through the townhouse to find Sebastian.

Valtina found him sitting in his study, attempting to focus on depositions for his upcoming trial. Like his wife, he was distracted by thoughts and feelings he didn't understand. Valtina entered his mind. "It's just a phase," he was assuring himself. "All married couples go through stuff like this. It will pass. We've always had such a hot sex life. We were bound to hit a dry spell at some point." But Valtina could tell that he didn't believe his own reassurances. He was now no more attracted to Claudia than she was to him.

Valtina thought this may be her easiest job yet. With the trickster gone, the couple was sure to part on their own. She wondered why Ladaya hadn't waited until the couple had already split. It seemed all there was for her to do was to sit back and wait until the couple parted. Then she could match them with their soul-mates. Valtina returned to the living room, sat on the couch, and watched television with Claudia for the rest of the day.

Much to Valtina's surprise, the couple carried on as usual on Saturday night and Sunday. They slept curled together in bed, they got up early and attended morning mass, and they dined at the same restaurant they always visited for Sunday brunch. It wasn't until later Sunday afternoon, when Claudia received a phone call from her father that things started to change. Valtina entered her mind, hoping to hear both sides of the conversation. But instead of being able to hear Claudia's father's words, all Valtina heard was the fear and terror in Claudia's mind. "I have to get over this… I have to find a way to make it work with Sebastian… Daddy will never understand… I don't think I could take the lectures from him if I ended things. What would happen to the firm?" Valtina left Claudia's mind… she'd heard all she needed to know. She entered Sebastian's mind and heard similar thoughts about both of their fathers. Valtina realized then why she'd been sent so soon… neither member of the couple would risk their fathers' wrath without some serious inspiration.

Valtina consulted her trusty leather satchel, looking for tools to aid her in her mission. The contents of the satchel changed with every mission. This time she found a college yearbook, a flyer for an art show, and a coupon for free admittance to a local club. Valtina's powers told her that the yearbook and the coupon should be left for Claudia, while the flyer would inspire Sebastian. She spilled a large box in Claudia's closet and placed the yearbook on top of the pile. Then, Valtina placed the flyer in Sebastian's briefcase… the coupon she would hold on to for now.

As Valtina had hoped, Claudia found the yearbook when she went to put away her shoes and lay out clothes for the next day. Valtina felt a sadness wash over Claudia, who quickly hid the book beneath her robe. She poked her head into Sebastian's study on her way to the couple's library.

If you enjoyed this sample then look for **Salvaged Soul Mates - The Leather Satchel Romance Series, Book 4.**

Other Books by Darla Dunbar

- The Romeo Alpha BBW Paranormal Shifter Romance Series

- Romeo Alpha Blood Lines Romance

- The Alpha Feud BBW Paranormal Shifter Romance Series

- The Alpha Packed BBW Paranormal Shifter Romance Series

- The Mind Talker Paranormal Romance Series

- The Leather Satchel Paranormal Romance Series

Get the latest update on new releases from the author at:

https://darladunbar.com/newsletter/

About the Author - Darla Dunbar

Darla has been interested in paranormal romance since she was a teenager in high school. It was then that she discovered she could fulfill her fantasies through her writing.

Observing people and human behavior in the area of romance has always been one of her favorite pastimes. Combining that with an overactive imagination is a sure fire way of coming up with interesting themes.

Connect with Darla Dunbar

I really appreciate you reading my book! Here are my social media coordinates:

Friend me on Facebook: https://www.facebook.com/darladunbar/

Follow me on Twitter: https://twitter.com/DarlDunbar

Check me out on Goodreads: https://www.goodreads.com/author/show/8425857.Darl a_Dunbar

Subscribe to my newsletter: https://darladunbar.com/newsletter/

Visit my website: https://darladunbar.com/

www.ingramcontent.com/pod-product-compliance
Lightning Source LLC
Chambersburg PA
CBHW030825200726
48288CB00004B/1400